CHRISTMAS COOKIE MYSTERY

BOOKS BY NAOMI MILLER

Blueberry Cupcake Mystery

Christmas Cookie Mystery

Lemon Tart Mystery
(Spring 2017)

Pumpkin Pie Mystery
(Fall 2017)

ENDORSEMENTS

"I'm ready to pull up a chair in The Sweet Shop, savor a slice of cinnamon bread, and dig into this juicy mystery."

~ Dana Mentink – multi published, award-winning author

"*Blueberry Cupcake Mystery*" is a warm and cozy mystery just right for reading in one sitting. This short novella is sweet in more ways than one and will not only whet your appetite for a bit of mystery but might just tempt your taste buds with its descriptions of The Sweet Shop's offerings."

~ Vine Voice

"A sweet, refreshing novella that will satisfy your sweet tooth as you weave your way through the crumbs to find the *"whodunit"*."

~ Amazon Reviewer

CHRISTMAS COOKIE MYSTERY

BY
NAOMI MILLER

Christmas Cookie Mystery
Copyright © 2016 by Naomi Miller

Christmas Cookie Mystery / Naomi Miller

ISBN: 978-0998169200 (Paperback)
ISBN: 978-1536531183 (eBook)
ASIN: B01LVW9MHD

1. Fiction / Religion & Spirituality / Christian Books & Bibles / Christian Fiction. 2. Fiction / Mystery, Thriller & Suspense / Mystery / Cozy. 3. Fiction / Christian Books & Bibles / Literature & Fiction / Amish & Mennonite.

2016938044

S&G Publishing, Knoxville, TN
www.sgpublish.com

All rights reserved. No part of this publication may be reproduced or transmitted for commercial purposes, without written permission of the publisher, except for brief quotations in printed reviews. Scripture quotations are from the Holy Bible (KJV)

This book is a work of fiction. Names, characters, places, and incidents are either products of the author's imagination or used fictitiously. Any similarity to actual people, organizations, and/or events is purely coincidental

Cover design ©Expresso Designs

First Edition 2016

To God be the Glory...

A NOTE FROM NAOMI MILLER

I love reading Amish fiction! I feel the Lord is calling me to write Amish fiction that is fun to read; free from the usual stress, anxiety, and other stomach-tightening reactions. Instead, I'm hoping to instill good feelings, good emotions, and good reactions.

I have created fictional characters, in a fictional town. As with any work of fiction, I've taken license in some areas of research as a means of creating circumstances necessary to my characters or plot. Any inaccuracies in the Amish, Mennonite or English lifestyles portrayed in this book are completely due to fictional license.

God bless you!

~Naomi

GLOSSARY

The German/Dutch dialect spoken by the Amish is not a written language. It is solely dependent on the location and origin of each settlement. The spellings below are approximations.

allrecht = all right
appeditlich = delicious
bruder/bruders = brother/brothers
buwe/buwes = boy/boys
danki = thank you
Dat = dad
dochder = daughter
du bischt daheem = you're home
Englischer = non-Amish person
freind/freinden = friend/friends
frau = wife
froh = happy
Gott = God
hochmut = pride

in lieb = in love
jah = yes
kaffe = coffee
kichlin = kitchen
kinner = children
kumme = come
maedel/maedels = girl/girls
Mamm = mom
naerfich = nervous
nee = no
rumschpringe = running around time for youth
schweschder/schweschders = sister/sisters
verrickt = crazy
wunderbaar = wonderful

And she shall bring forth a son,

and thou shall call his name JESUS:

for he shall save his people from their sins.

Matthew 1:21

For Rachel

ONE

Katie Chupp felt more than a little guilty as she climbed the ladder . . .

Dear Lord, please don't let this be something I'll regret. . . please allow gut to kumme from it. Let it be a blessing to someone.

In all her seventeen years, she had never taken part in such an activity before, although she had been giving it a lot of thought for some time now. And if she was to be perfectly honest about it, she had wanted the chance to do something about it.

Ach, what would Mamm think if she knew? Would she or Dat approve of what I'm doing right now? Or would they tell me to—

"You're looking awful nervous there, Katie. Are you certain you won't get into all kinds of trouble?"

Katie looked down at Travis Davis, who was holding her ladder steady. Travis had begun working at the Sweet Shop in July, after he returned home to find that his siblings had ransacked the bakery where Katie worked.

After insisting that his brothers help to return the bakery to its' pristine condition, Mrs. Simpkins had admonished them to never do such a thing again. Then she had insisted on giving Travis a part-time job at the bakery, until such time that he could find full-time work.

Clearing his throat, he continued. "I don't think your parents would approve. And you might even get in trouble with the church!

I'm pretty sure those older dudes who make the rules your family has to follow would frown on this. They might throw you out of the church!" Travis looked troubled, as he held tightly to the ladder.

"*Ach*, that is not going to happen, Travis. You worry too much. If someone from the community finds out, I can always blame it on my *rumschpringe*." Katie said, stopping halfway up the ladder. She glanced down again at the handsome young man.

Katie had caught herself looking at Travis on more than one occasion. She hadn't shared with anyone—even her best *freinden*—how often he seemed to drift into her thoughts.

So what if I like him! And so what if I find him cute . . . and exciting . . . and being with him makes me feel more than a wee bit dangerous. This is what my rumschpringe is for . . . to consider things outside the Ordnung, so that I can make a gut decision -

an informed decision – based on what I really want. Everyone knows I will choose baptism. And that will be the end of it.

Giving him a smile, she reached for the spray can, but Travis refused to let go. Pulling it just out of her reach, he tried again.

"Katie, I'm serious. You don't have to do this. Just think about the consequences. You could get in a lot of trouble. Mrs. Simpkins might be forced to fire you."

"*Nee*, Travis. I've never had an opportunity to do something like this before, and I refuse to let anything—or anyone—stop me. Now, hand me that spray can."

She added, with a smile, "You wouldn't want to be responsible for allowing me to fall off this ladder, would you?"

"Okay, okay. Here. Take it. But don't blame me if something bad happens."

Katie giggled, as she shook the can. "*Nee*. I won't be blaming you . . . unless you shake the ladder and ruin my work."

Turning back to the window, Katie concentrated on the almost-invisible lines she had drawn before Travis arrived with the supplies she had requested. She had asked Travis to buy the things she needed, knowing he would not draw any suspicion.

"For sure and for certain, this may be the most fun I have ever had." Leaning forward on the ladder, Katie began spraying the window near the top left corner. "And besides, who would be around to catch us? All the stores are closed now."

"I just wish I had thought to cover the windows on the outside with brown paper, so no one could see what we're doing." Travis looked around, as if he knew someone was watching them.

"Stop worrying. We'll be done soon and on our way home. Now take this, and hand me the green one." Katie handed Travis the spray can she had been using. After she took the newly offered spray can, she began shaking it as vigorously as she had the first one. Then she leaned around the side of the ladder and began spraying short, straight lines of green paint all along a large section of the window.

* * *

It didn't take as long as Katie had thought it would to finish it. Less than three hours later, Katie and Travis were carrying all the supplies to the back, where they stored them in an unused closet, which mostly held cleaning supplies.

After Travis put the ladder back in it's place, Katie found a spot on a nearby shelf for the spray paint cans. As she turned to leave, she noticed a paper bag on the lower shelf.

"Have you noticed this bag before? Is it something you brought with you?"

"I've never seen it before," replied Travis. "I wonder if it had supplies that you could have used on the window."

Katie pulled the bag out, where she could see into it.

"*Ach*! What is this doing here?"

"What is it? Can I see?"

Katie knew she had to say something, but she wasn't sure if this was something Travis should be told. "I am thinking that Mrs. Simpkins has hidden something in here that she's purchased for a Christmas gift. To be honest, I didn't expect to find something like this hidden at the back of the shelf. For sure, she must have some secret plans for it. Please don't say anything to the others."

"Don't worry! I won't say anything about it." As he peeked into the bag, Katie saw his eyes widen and a whistle escaped his lips. "Oh man, I did not expect that!"

Katie rushed to speak. "I just know there's a *gut* reason for it. I cannot imagine Mrs. Simpkins buying this for herself."

"I think you're right about it being a

Christmas gift for someone. Put it back where you found it. Then I'll drive you home. There's no need for you to call for a ride."

Before she could answer, Travis leaned forward and put his arms around her. As he pulled her close in a hug, it made her feel *wunderbaar*—but she knew her *mamm* and *dat* would not approve. After a minute, she pulled away from him.

When he smiled at her, Katie's heart seemed to soar. Her legs felt shaky as she felt the heat rush into her cheeks. This might not be the first time she had been attracted to this young man, but she was smart enough to know her feelings for him were changing.

There was only one problem. . . Travis was an *Englischer*.

Dear Lord, don't let me make a mistake—or give Travis the wrong idea. Please help me to know what to do about this new development. . .

On the First Day of Christmas . . .

Frosted Christmas Cookies

Cookie Ingredients:
- 1 1/2 cups sugar
- 1 1/2 cups butter
- 1 3/4 cups shortening
- 1/2 teaspoon salt
- 1 tsp pure vanilla extract
- 1 tsp pure almond extract
- 1 large egg
- 8 1/2 cups plain flour

Frosting Ingredients:
- 2 cups confectioner's sugar
- 1/2 teaspoon pure almond extract
- pinch of salt
- 3-4 tablespoons milk

NAOMI MILLER

Instructions:

1. Mix together sugar, butter, shortening, salt and vanilla until smooth and creamy
2. Add egg. Mix together, scraping sides of bowl
3. Add flour, mixing only long enough to combine
4. Divide dough into several balls, each the size of a baseball
5. Wrap dough in plastic wrap and refrigerate until dough is chilled
6. Form each ball into a long roll, 1inch in diameter
7. Refrigerate wrapped dough again until cold.
8. When ready, remove a roll from the refrigerator and cut into 1/2" thick slices. Place cut side up on a lightly greased cookie sheet. Make indentation in center of each cookie to hold spot of icing
9. Bake at 350° about 8-10 minutes, until edges begin to slightly turn golden brown
10. Cool completely on the baking sheet

CHRISTMAS COOKIE MYSTERY

Frosting Instructions:

1. Mix together sugar, almond extract, salt and milk
2. Continue to add milk 1 tablespoon at a time until icing is desired consistency
3. Dab a small bit of frosting into each indentation

TWO

"Katie, are you smelling your hands again? I told you to stop worrying about it."

"I can't seem to help it. I didn't know I would end up with the smell of paint on me. I guess I should have used the plastic gloves we use in the bakery when we're handling the food. Even after washing my hands twice, I can still smell the paint."

Katie sniffed her hands again, before looking over at Travis, only to find him watching her. They both started laughing.

After they had finished putting everything away and locked up, Katie had planned to call Mr. Baker, her family's usual driver, but Travis had insisted on taking her home.

"*Danki, Travis,* for driving me home. I didn't mean to act like I didn't want you to drive me home. "

"It's okay. I shouldn't have insisted on it. I'm still practically a stranger."

"But you're also my *freind. Danki* for understanding—and for your forgiveness." Katie smiled, and then suddenly reached up with her hand to smack her head. "*Ach*, I forgot to ask you about your family. How is your *mamm* doing? Is everything going well for her now?"

"Yes, everyone is doing well. Mom's recovery might be slow, but she is recovering." Travis glanced over at Katie, then back at the road.

"I want to talk about the window. I think

anyone who sees it will be amazed. You have a real talent for art." He shook his head at his own comment and Katie wanted to ask him what he was thinking, but held her tongue.

Is it really so ridiculous that a plain girl could be talented with a can of spray paint?

She nearly giggled at the picture that formed in her mind. "Isn't that what *Englischers* consider 'tagging'?"

"Nope, definitely not. Tagging is when someone sneaks and paints a picture—or a message—on a wall for everyone to see."

"And isn't that just what I did tonight?" Katie giggled again.

"No. It's not the same. Mrs. Simpkins will love it." Travis signaled a left turn and slowed almost to a stop, before turning onto the familiar dirt road. "On the other hand, I still think you could get into trouble if anyone from your church finds out it was you who did it."

Glancing over at Katie, he grinned. "And stop smelling your hands! If you don't stop, you'll give it away. Everyone will know it was you!"

Katie tucked her hands under her legs. With a giggle, she sat back and tried to calm her fluttering heart. Whether it was the activity at the bakery, or the company—or both—she felt more than a little reckless tonight.

Is this wrong, Gott? Am I straying too far from the way I was brought up? Would Mamm and Dat be ashamed of me? Is it wrong to have feelings for Travis? He's my freind. He's just my freind. Nothing more . . .

* * *

Katie asked Travis to let her out at a side road near her home, knowing if she cut across the field, she could make it home in time for dinner. Although she had been careful to wash them not just once, but twice, she thought she could still detect the strange odor on her fingers.

Of course, no one at home would probably notice. And if anyone did, she could say it was from working on a surprise for Christmas. Even her *mamm* and *dat* would usually not require further explanations when this excuse was used.

As she walked along, she looked around their farm. Although *hochmut* was something the preachers spoke against, Katie always felt something akin to it whenever she thought of her home and everything her *dat* had worked hard to accomplish.

Caleb Chupp was a *gut* man, who was respected and admired by most all the families in Abbott Creek. Caleb taught his children to love the Lord and put others first, something the *Englisch* community had turned into an acronym. As if a person needed to use the word 'JOY' to remind themselves to put Jesus first, others second, and yourself last.

NAOMI MILLER

The Chupp farm was neat, clean, and appeared prosperous. Katie's *dat* and elder *bruder* Ervin worked hard from sunup to sundown. Katie's other *bruders*, Noah and Caleb might be younger than her, but they were expected to do their share of chores.

Noah also worked as an apprentice in town for a local craftsman, Samuel Miller, who made buggies for plain folk, and even some *Englischers*.

Caleb had two more years of school, so he had fewer chores to do. Morning chores had to be done before breakfast. After school, he was diligent to change back into his choring clothes and head outside to finish up before suppertime.

Katie caught sight of her *dat* coming out of the barn, and ran over to meet him. She laughed as he swatted at her with his straw hat.

"Katie-girl, *did you kumme* to help with the choring? If you did, you *should have kumme* sooner. The *buwes* have already finished and are washing up for supper."

"*Nee*, I stayed late to work on something for Mrs. Simpkins. I'm just now getting home. I thought I might walk back to the house with you."

"In that case, I'm mighty glad for your company. Since you began working at that bakery, I don't get to see you as often as I did."

"*Dat*, you didn't see me any more before than you do now; I was in school all day."

"Well, that might be right, but with you growing up before my eyes, it for sure seems like I see less of you. And I'm *froh* to have your company."

* * *

When Katie and her *dat* walked into the *kichlin*, her *mamm* was filling glasses on the table with milk.

"Katie, *du bischt daheem*. What has kept you so late? You almost missed your supper.

I was about to send your *dat* to look for you."

"*Mamm*, I told you I was going to stay late and work on a surprise for Mrs. Simpkins. You should not have held supper for me. I am all grown up now. You do not have to worry about me."

"Now, Katie. Your *dat* and I agreed to have supper a little late tonight, in case you made it home in time to eat with the family. And no matter how grown up my *kinner* get, I always fret a bit. I know that *Gott* is looking out for you, but I'm still your *mamm*—and you're still my *dochder*—and I will always worry about you."

Katie's *mamm* gathered her close for a hug. Martha Chupp had been raised in a home where hugs were scarce, but she had always given her *kinner* lots of hugs.

"*Mamm*, do you need me to help prepare the food for the Sunday gathering? I'll have time after supper to help with whatever needs to be done."

"Well, if you could bake a couple of pies, I think everything else has already been done. Do you think you will have time after supper?"

"Of course. I'm glad there's something left for me to do. I want to do my share of the work, you know."

Katie moved to where *Mamm* had set out glasses. She gathered them up to move them to the long table. As she looked around to see what else needed doing, she watched her *Dat,* as he moved over to stand behind *Mamm,* who was still standing at the stove and tended to supper.

She could still remember how *Mamm* had told each of the *kinner* on their first day of school that she would always make time for hugs—no matter how old they got. Even now, Ervin, who was nineteen and seemed all grown up, always gave his *mamm* a hug before he went up to his bedroom at night.

Her thoughts were interrupted by a laugh

from *Mamm* as she swatted at *Dat* with her spatula.

"Caleb Chupp, you are likely to have no dinner if you insist on distracting me." *Mamm* laughed again as *Dat* reached out to grab hold of the spatula, then swooped in for a kiss. When he stepped back, he was smiling at *Mamm*.

"Iffen I have to choose between my *frau* and my supper, I'll choose you over supper any day of the week."

Katie sighed. *That's what I want. . . I want someone to be in lieb with me—and kiss me—and make me smile, like Dat does with Mamm.*

Mamm turned to Katie, but there was still a big smile on her face as she said, "Go call your *bruders* and *schweschders* to supper, Katie."

On the Second Day of Christmas . . .

Ginger Snap Cookies

Ingredients:
- 3/4 cup shortening
- 1 cup sugar
- 1 large egg
- 1/3 cup molasses
- 2 1/3 cups sifted flour
- 2 teaspoons baking soda
- 1 teaspoon ginger
- 1 teaspoon cinnamon
- 1/2 teaspoon cloves
- 1/4 teaspoon salt
- Extra sugar as needed for dipping

Instructions:
1. Cream shortening and sugar together
2. Add molasses and beaten egg
3. Add spices to sifted flour along with baking soda and salt
4. Add dry ingredients to creamed mixture

5. Shape dough into one-inch balls and dip in sugar
6. Place on a lightly greased cookie sheet
7. Bake in 350° oven for 15–18 minutes
8. *Remove from pan and place on rack to cool*

THREE

Travis braced himself as he opened the door, knowing that Bobby, his little brother, was likely to be just on the other side, waiting to throw himself at his older brother.

No pint-sized bullet hit him as he stepped through the doorway into the front hall. He stood there a moment, shaking his head, as he looked into the empty living room. There were a few toys dropped haphazardly around the floor, but no Bobby.

It took only a step further down the hall for Travis to realize he could hear voices coming from the back of the little house. He followed the sounds, taking note of the dinner dishes piled neatly beside the sink to be washed.

Is it my night for dish duty? It must be. If it were Gwen's turn, she would have done them by now. He let out a small sigh at the thought of having to scrub dishes for a dinner he had missed altogether.

I shouldn't complain. Mrs. Simpkins didn't have to pay me to stay tonight, but she had insisted. I would have stayed whether she'd paid me or not. I couldn't have left Katie up on that ladder all by herself.

Travis worried much more about Katie than he ought to. The very thought of her up on the ladder with no one else there with her, had him clenching his teeth together as he set down the box of desserts and breads Katie had handed him on his way out the door.

She had insisted the bread was old and could not be sold—and the desserts were extras that would be too crisp to sell the next day. And, while he knew that Mrs. Simpkins preferred they sell fresh desserts and breads, he did not buy Katie's insistence that it was accidental.

He was beginning to worry, quite a bit, about his growing feelings for Katie.

The hug. . . That hug had been totally unplanned, and probably a huge mistake. She had pulled away after only a minute, but those sixty seconds—give or take a few—had been enough to give him plenty to worry about.

Hopefully, she hasn't noticed yet how much I care. But what are we going to do? It's not like she'd leave her church—and her family—for someone like me.

Pushing those thoughts aside for a moment, he remembered how much the whole town had gotten in on the act of caring for his family. There always seemed to be someone dropping off a casserole or a pie or a dozen cookies.

And that wasn't even counting the stuff Katie's community had brought them. Someone had actually left an enormous container of milk on the porch.

He'd opened the front door to leave for work one morning and there it was; a large, metal bottle or bucket—or whatever—of milk, with a note that said it was for the children . . . and cooking . . . and whatever else it was needed for.

Other families had brought eggs, bags of flour and sugar in sizes he hadn't even known a person could buy in stores, whole meals and more friendship bread than he thought the whole block could eat, but the younger kids didn't seem to have any trouble packing it away.

Even Bobby, who was only five, always

seemed to have food in his hands now. All of it was greatly appreciated, but Travis couldn't help but wonder just how much his mom had kept from him. Surely the kids wouldn't be eating like that if they'd had normal meals before.

They wouldn't have been stealing food, either. I must find out what's going on—and who's involved. I don't want anyone getting hurt, especially my family—or Katie.

He turned to leave the kitchen. Instead, he let out his breath in a huff when his little bullet of a brother rammed into him.

"Travis! You're home!"

"Yeah, buddy. I'm home."

Bobby was already peeking around his older brother to look inside the box Travis had put down on the counter.

"What'd you bring home? Did Katie make these? When is she gonna make some more of those yummy cupcakes? Oh WOW! Look at all this stuff!"

Travis chuckled as Bobby fired off questions, while rooting around in the box at the same time.

"I don't know why you always ask what's in the box rug-rat. You'll see it before I can tell you, anyway." He ruffled a hand through Bobby's hair, as his brother grunted a response.

"Now, to answer your other questions. Yes, Katie made most of the stuff in there, and I don't know when she's planning to make more cupcakes, but I can ask her tomorrow, when I see her."

Bobby started to speak, but changed his mind and nodded his head instead, while he stuffed his face with thick slices of raisin bread.

Oh well, at least he didn't start with the cookies.

"Hey pal, where is everybody else?"

Bobby waved a hand toward the back room of the house, but didn't try to speak again, with his mouth full of bread.

"Don't eat it all, ya hear." Travis let out a chuckle as Bobby turned toward him, a sneaky smile on his face.

"I mean it, Bobby. I know you've had dinner, but it's getting late. You don't need to go to bed with a full stomach."

A lightly muffled "k" was the only response Travis heard as he walked out of the kitchen.

The laughter he'd heard earlier grew louder as he moved down the hallway, one voice in particular standing out to him. Travis gritted his teeth and forced a smile onto his face.

When Katie had brought her boss and Mr. O'Neal with her on the fourth of July, he'd been certain the charming Irishman was involved with Mrs. Simpkins, but since the man had visited them more often than anyone else in town, Travis was beginning to think the cafe owner had designs on his mother.

Any concerns he had about the age difference aside, Travis knew his mother was not ready for anything romantic. It had not even been a year since his father's passing.

He squared his shoulders and prepared to force himself to be polite as he approached the open doorway of the den, where his mother spent most of her time. She had finally begun to recover from her bout with pneumonia—and then the weather had turned cold, bringing with it the possibility of a myriad of other infections.

Even a simple cold could be devastating for her right now.

The sight that met him was not at all what he had expected—and yet much worse.

Gwen was sitting way too close to a young man who bore a striking resemblance to Mr. O'Neal. The young man was gesturing wildly and spinning an obviously tall tale for Gwen, their mother, and his two brothers.

"So, did he kiss it?"

"He did indeed, lass. He kissed the blarney stone full on, he did. He had a wager to win."

Gwen collapsed in giggles; while Travis watched his younger brothers make faces. That told him there had been something disgusting about the story.

"Tis the truth. . . honest."

Travis looked up at the sound of Mr. O'Neal's voice. Indeed, he was here, and not only was he flirting outrageously, but the man's obvious relative. . . son, cousin, nephew. . . was clearly after his own little sister.

"Travis! When did you get home?" Gwen spoke up, rushing over to pull Travis into the room with everyone. "You have to hear this story. It's hilarious. Go on, please tell it again, Sean."

"Alas, t'would be my pleasure, but I see how late the hour is. I believe we should be going now."

"Aye; we really should be goin' on now."

Travis restrained himself as the two quick-talking Irishmen rose to say their goodbyes. He really wanted to make some sort of show of annoyance, but he had a sense that it would not go over well with his sister . . . or his mother, for that matter, so he kept it to himself.

Gwen offered to walk their two visitors to the door—and Travis followed, stopping in the kitchen only because he spotted Bobby stuffing yet another treat into his mouth.

"Okay kid, that's enough. You keep that up, you're going to end up with a stomach ache."

"Aww, come on, Travis."

"No, you come on, little brother. It's time for you to start getting ready for bed."

Bobby dragged his feet all the way to the bathroom, only moving through the doorway after Travis gave him a slight push in the right direction. "Go on, now. Brush your teeth."

"Night, Travis." Mr. O'Neal called from the front hall, a moment before he pulled his younger relative through the doorway.

Travis stood beside the bathroom door, watching as the two made their way down the broken and crooked walkway that led from the front door to the street.

He expected Gwen to shut the door and turn, but she stayed where she was.

She must have been watching them walk away, too.

On the Third Day of Christmas . . .

Irish Shortbread Cookies

Ingredients:
- 1 cup butter
- 2/3 cup sugar
- 1/2 cup cornstarch
- 2 cups flour

Instructions:
1. Cream butter and sugar together until light and fluffy
2. Sift in cornstarch and flour; mix well
3. Press into 10 ¾ x 7 inch pan
4. Prick all over with a fork
5. Bake in preheated oven 275° for 30 minutes, then reduce heat to 250 F and bake 1 – 1-1/2 hours longer
6. Remove from pan and sprinkle with powdered sugar
7. Cut into 20 tube-shaped cookies

FOUR

Katie followed her *Mamm* into the Yoder *kichlin*. They each carried a basket of food and a pie. Katie felt silly carrying the food. It felt as if she was telling everyone she had made it . . . she still felt guilty that she had been so excited over Mrs. Simpkins' window art. As a matter of fact, after everything that happened at the bakery, she had nearly forgotten about preparations for church the next day.

"There she is."

Katie turned her head at the familiar voice and saw Ida Yoder walking over to take the basket from *Mamm's* hands.

"Katie, we have been looking forward to one of your pies for two weeks now."

"*Danki*, but I am afraid this is not one of mine. *Mamm* asked me to bake a couple of pies, then she surprised me after supper—with two pies she had made before I got home from the bakery."

Mamm clucked her tongue before adding, "I may not have your touch for baking, Katie, but I used your recipe at least."

"*Ach*, then it will be just the same. Katie certainly got her baking skills from you, Martha."

Katie's *mamm* waved away the compliment, but Katie was grateful for the distraction and nearly made her escape—until Ida moved over to put an arm around her shoulders.

"Amelia Simpkins works you so hard. Whatever will she do when you find a young man who convinces you it is time for your *rumschpringe* to be finished and done with, so you can join the church and marry?"

Katie blushed furiously at the thought which immediately came to mind. Fortunately, Ida and *Mamm* took her reddened cheeks to mean something else entirely.

"Ida, you shouldn't tease Katie so. She is only seventeen. She has plenty of time to find a young man."

Ida laughed before adding, "Right you are. And for sure and for certain she will appreciate having some money saved when the time *kummes*." She squeezed Katie's shoulders again before letting go and moving on to relieve another of their food for the afternoon meal.

"Just be sure you *kumme* to the singing this Wednesday, Katie."

"I will do my best." And with that, Katie made her escape.

She was certain *Mamm* said something to Ida as she was moving away, but it was much too loud in the busy *kichlin* to hear her clearly—and Katie did not stop to listen, anyway.

She could tell herself all she wanted that she must find a young man in the community who held her fancy, but at the same time, she was troubled when the only young man who came to mind, was the one who had held her attention of late.

Katie had no more than stepped off the porch in the direction of the barn, than Freida looped an arm through hers.

"Isn't it a beautiful, *wunderbaar* morning, Katie!"

Katie could not help but smile at her *freind's* enthusiasm. Freida was one of those young *maedels* who would always be happy in spirit.

"It is indeed, Freida."

"You will be at the singing this week, *jah*?"

Katie mumbled a hmm, but Freida didn't seem to notice a lack of response. When her footsteps slowed as they crossed the yard, Katie followed the direction her *freind* was looking. She was not a bit surprised that the group of young men Freida was watching contained several of the Yoder *buwes*.

"One of these days I am going to find out just which *buwe* you are interested in."

Freida turned back to Katie, her cheeks stained a deep pink. "For sure and for certain, I do not know what you could be talking about, Katie Chupp."

Her insistence, coupled with the deep pink of her cheeks tickled Katie's sense of humor—and it only took a moment for Freida to join in and they were both laughing.

When Katie caught the expression on Lizzy Yoder's hard features, she stifled her giggles and shushed Freida. The two of them moved away from the crowd as they struggled to reign in their amusement.

"Katie Chupp, you are likely to get us both in such trouble."

"Me. . . It is not me who was telling tales, Freida Schmidt."

"What are you two giggling over?" Katie's younger sister, Leah, appeared in front of them, looking very much like *Mamm*, with her disapproving look—which set Katie off again.

Then they were both struggling again with giggles that threatened to erupt and promised to get them both into trouble with the church elders.

"Little *schweschder*, you will understand soon enough. I assure you of that."

"I will never understand why you would want to get in trouble on a day of worship." And with a "hmph" at the two of them, Leah went off to walk into the barn with the other young *maedels*.

"I am going to enjoy watching her, when she discovers *buwes*."

Katie grinned, as she answered. "I am not certain she will ever be one to giggle and act silly. . . not even over a *buwe*. She will just find one who is as serious as she is—and they will go on the same way."

"Oh Katie, *kumme* now, you cannot know that. She may well surprise you. She could end up very different than she acts now."

"You might be right, but I doubt it." She nearly laughed again at the very idea, but she managed to stifle it as *Dat* and the other elders walked by them, making their way into the barn.

"*Kumme* Freida, we had better get to our seats."

"*Jah*, we can always talk later, after the meal."

Arm in arm, the two of them followed the group moving through the wide-open barn doors, separating only when they reached the row where Katie's *mamm* and *schweschders* were already seated.

Katie took the seat on the end of the row, knowing she would need to scoot out quickly to go and help prepare the meal as soon as service was finished.

On the Fourth Day of Christmas . . .

Pecan Drop Cookies

Ingredients:
- 2 large eggs
- 3/4 cup sugar
- 1 cup butter
- 1 cup pecans, chopped
- 1 teaspoon pure vanilla extract
- 1/2 teaspoon pure almond extract
- 2 cups plain flour
- 1/4 teaspoon baking powder
- 1/2 teaspoon salt

Instructions:
1. Preheat oven to 350°
2. Combine flour, salt, and baking powder
3. Mix butter and sugar at high speed until light and fluffy
4. Add egg, and mix until well blended
5. Add vanilla extract

6. Reduce mixer speed to low
7. Add flour mixture; mix just until combined
8. Stir in pecans
9. Shape dough into a 4-inch round balls and cover with plastic wrap
10. Chill for 1 hour
11. Roll dough to 1/4 inch thickness on a lightly floured surface
11. Cut out 40 (2 x 3 inch) cookies, re-rolling scraps as necessary
12. Place cookies 1 inch apart on a baking sheet lined with parchment paper
13. Bake at 350° for 9 minutes or until lightly browned on bottoms
14. Cool on a wire rack
15. Dust cooled cookies with powdered sugar

FIVE

The next morning, Katie held tight to the basket that *Mamm* had given her as she was preparing to leave for the bakery.

Her pace this morning was much quicker than usual. Her feet struggled to keep up with the excitement that had taken hold of her before she'd even made it out of bed this morning.

Dat would certainly tell her she was being prideful, but Katie could not seem to make the fluttery excitement in her stomach go away. She was excited to see what the town would think of the new décor in the bakery window. And although he had seen them the night before, Katie could hardly wait to see what Travis thought of them in the light of day.

Thinking about the bakery reminded Katie of the bag she and Travis had found in the closet.

Why does Mrs. Simpkins have it—and why did she hide it in the closet?

Scooting a bit further away from the road when she heard the rumble of an engine from behind her, Katie looked down at the basket she carried and kept thinking about the display at the Sweet Shop.

"Katie!"

She looked up as a familiar voice called out to her from the car that was slowing down beside her.

"Travis! It is early. Are you already on your way to the Sweet Shop?"

"Not yet. I have a few things to take care

of in the city, but I wondered if you might want a ride to work since I have to go right through town."

Katie vigorously nodded her head and moved to get into the car. She felt a little shiver of excitement when Travis reached across the seat and opened the door for her, and again when he pushed the seat forward for her to put the large basket she carried in the back seat.

Ach, he is always so thoughtful.

She set the basket down carefully and then moved back as Travis pushed the seat back into place for her.

When she was settled in the seat beside him, Travis turned to her again. "How can you walk so far every morning? Aren't you freezing?"

When Katie shrugged and then shivered, Travis pulled a blanket she had not even noticed out of the backseat and handed it to her.

"Here. Wrap up in that. You'll be warm in no time."

Katie wasted no time in spreading the blanket out over her legs and pulled it up to cover her arms. She was accustomed to the chilly walk from home, but it was a nice change to be warm on the ride to town.

Travis turned his attention to driving while Katie chatted and soon they were speeding over the narrow country lane toward town.

Katie pulled the blanket up to her face, breathing in the scent that hung over it like the aroma of cookies and cakes that filled the Sweet Shop whenever she was baking.

The smells from the blanket reminded her of the family she had recently met; the little boy who had insisted his big brother would fix everything, the young girl who had answered the front door with timid eyes and a hesitant smile, the mother who had radiated love—even from her sickbed, and the young man himself. With a blush, Katie remembered the hug Travis had given her on Saturday night.

Travis is indeed blessed with a wunderbaar family. He didn't mean anything by the hug. He's my freind.

"Do you think Mrs. Simpkins will like the window?" Katie tried to sound casual, as if she was just making conversation, but she couldn't help looking over at Travis as she spoke, hoping for a positive reaction.

He did not disappoint. Before she even finished her question, she could see a smile pull the corners of his mouth up.

"I don't think it's just Mrs. Simpkins you're wondering about, Katie."

Katie busied herself looking out at the countryside that whipped past the window beside her, but looked back at him a moment later when she heard a low chuckle.

"I think the whole town will love it. It has something for everyone. You did an excellent job."

"*Danki*." She ducked her head as relief washed over her.

Gut. He is not laughing at me. She turned to speak again, but stopped when she saw they were already at the edge of town.

"Well, Katie I do believe you are going to be early." Travis smiled as he looked over at her.

"*Jah*. It's *gut*. I can get a head start on the baking."

"Just don't you work too hard. And don't go near that closet—or say anything to anyone, at least until I get back."

"*Nee*, I won't. Besides, I love baking." She took one last sniff of the warm blanket before carefully folding it up in her lap, just as Travis pulled into the Sweet Shop's small parking area.

"Well, I will see you later, then."

Katie smiled at the reminder. She had nearly forgotten that Travis would be working at the Sweet Shop later that afternoon. She would see him again soon.

"*Jah*, later. Drive safely, and take care in the city."

"Thanks. I will. Just a couple of quick things I need to see to. Then it's right back to Abbott Creek." He said no more, and though it was a struggle, Katie did not ask what business Travis had in the city. It was his to share if he felt the need—and clearly he had not, so it was not her place to ask.

She for sure and for certain did not need to be nosy about his personal business. She was already pushing her luck with what she kept trying to convince herself was only an innocent infatuation.

"*Danki* for the ride." She opened the heavy door and slid out of the low seat, turning to pull her basket from the back.

Travis had already moved the heavy seat forward for her, so all she had to do was lift the basket out. Once she did, she reached to close the door.

"Well, I'll see you this afternoon."

"*Jah*, this afternoon." She smiled at the thought that perhaps he was just as reluctant to leave, as she was to see him go.

She started to speak again, but a strong gust of wind came up from behind her, and the stark contrast of chilly air as opposed to the warmth that had settled over her, made her shiver.

"Katie, you'd better get inside. You've been in this warm car. You don't want to get sick. And take care of yourself."

"*Jah*, you're right. I will see you later, then." With that, she closed the door of his car and headed for the front door of the Sweet Shop.

As she unlocked the door, memories washed over her. She could remember well that morning all those months ago, when she had done this very thing—only to find a disaster awaiting her inside the Sweet Shop.

The bakery had been a mess! The display case was empty, except for a few crumbs and some broken pieces of decoration.

Some of the jams, preserves, butters and specialty items had been taken, although most were intact, still on the higher shelves, untouched.

But the lower shelves were pretty much empty. Dozens of loaves of bread, including favorites like whole wheat, pumpkin, cinnamon and zucchini, were missing.

Even many of the prepared orders, waiting to be picked up, were gone! Katie had been scared, but she had acted brave when her *freind* Freida showed up.

Katie had suggested they run across the street to The Coffee Cup, where she had contacted the owner, Mrs. Simpkins. They waited there until Mrs. Simpkins arrived, along with a police officer.

That mess had brought their community together in a way that none could have expected—starting with Travis and his family.

She had stumbled across the evidence completely by accident when she had met his youngest *bruder*. Of course she had done everything she could to help—and she was grateful that Mrs. Simpkins had come up with such a *wunderbaar* solution for the other two *bruders*.

Of course, the real surprise had been Katie's plain community. Even though they were always quick to help each other, she had not expected the outpouring of love they had shown the little Englisch family who had lost their *dat* only a few months before.

I should have, though. They are such *wunderbaar* people.

Now there was another mystery at the bakery—another mystery to solve. Katie knew Travis wanted her to wait for him, but if she had the chance to investigate a little, it couldn't hurt anything.

She looked back as she pushed open the door. Travis still sat there, waiting. With a laugh, she stepped inside the shop and gave the front room a good look, before she stepped back outside and waved a hand to him.

Travis returned the wave and then slowly pulled away. Once the red of his lights completely disappeared around the side of the building, Katie moved to go back inside.

Hearing a shout from nearby, she looked around. Hannah was crossing the street, heading toward the bakery.

"Katie, I am glad you are here early." Hannah's voice held a tone of relief.

Katie was surprised to see her *freind* so early in the day; normally around this time Hannah would be preparing to open The Coffee Cup.

"*Gut* morning, Hannah. What is it you need?"

"Our delivery of pastries never came last

night. Mr. Dell left me a note to fill in our own stock with whatever I can this morning. I am hoping you have lots of extra on hand. Oh, and I brought you a coffee—just the way you like it."

"*Danki* for the *kaffe*. But this is not the best time of year for us to have extras on hand." As Hannah's hopeful expression disappeared, Katie could not help but think of the basket she had sent with Travis the night before.

Certainly Hannah would not have wanted the day-old pastries that were left over. And then she remembered that, thanks to Travis driving her to work, now she was nearly forty minutes early.

"Wait! I got here early today, so I have nearly an extra hour this morning. I can certainly make up some extra pastries in all that time. Is there anything specific you are needing?"

A smile spread across Hannah's face as

she reached out and took hold of Katie's hands.

"Katie, you are a life saver. I have a list of what we sell the most. Any of them would be a help." She handed the list over. As Katie looked down at the half dozen items on the list, she breathed a sigh of relief. Most of the things would be simple to make and quick to bake.

"Oh, and we have been selling out every day of those *wunderbaar* flaky croissants. You know the ones."

Katie nodded her head. She had been experimenting with her own version of them ever since Hannah had brought her one.

"Tis a *gut* thing I have been working on a similar recipe for the bakery. I cannot promise these will taste just like what Mr. Dell orders, but I will do my best."

"Dear Katie, your best is so much better than us having nothing. *Danki*. Mr. Dell will for sure be pleased."

"Well, I had better get to work, then."

"*Jah. Danki*, Katie. You just give me a call when the first batch is ready. I'll run right over and get them."

"*Jah*, I will, Hannah. And *danki* again for the *appeditlich kaffe*." With that, Katie gave her *freind* a quick hug. Then, opening the door, she went back inside the bakery—while Hannah looked both ways before crossing the street and heading back to the Coffee Cup.

Don't work too hard, indeed. Katie nearly laughed aloud at the thought.

On the Fifth Day of Christmas . . .

Christmas Date Cookies
Kid Friendly Recipe

Ingredients:

    2 large eggs

    4 cups rice cereal

    1 1/2 cups chopped dates

    1 tablespoon butter

    2 cups sugar

    1 bag coconut (optional)

Instructions:

    1. Add eggs, dates, butter and sugar to medium pot

    2. Cook together 5-15 minutes or until the mixture pulls away from the pan

    3. Pour over rice cereal

    4. Roll into balls and coat with coconut

SIX

"Katie, what are you doing?" Freida's surprised voice caught her unaware. Katie jumped and the mixing bowl in her hand skidded away from her.

Both Katie and Freida scrambled to catch the bowl as it spun around in a circle on the counter and nearly toppled over, splashing the ingredients up and around the sides as it turned.

"I've got it." Freida reached for the bowl just as Katie touched the rim. The opposing forces sent the bowl and its ingredients spinning out of reach, batter spilling across the workstation between the two *maedels*.

Katie looked up at Freida and both girls looked around at the unusually messy *kichlin*—and then burst into fits of laughter.

Several times they tried to say something—and every time, they both began speaking at the same time, which only made them laugh all the harder.

It was several minutes before the laughter quieted enough for Katie to clear her throat a bit and try again to speak, without interrupting her *freind*.

Freida was quicker this time though. "Katie, I am so very sorry, but really, what are you doing? You could not have waited for me to do the morning baking?"

Katie laughed once more before she was able to calm herself enough to answer. "Actually Freida, this is not the usual morning baking."

When Freida opened her mouth to interrupt, Katie pushed on. "I got here early, which must have been a part of *Gott's* plan, because I had barely opened the door, when Hannah rushed over and asked if we could make some extra pastries for the Coffee Cup this morning."

Katie waited a moment before going on, giving Freida time to say something—but she said nothing.

"Their pastry delivery never arrived yesterday and they are out of the morning pastries that the customers will be expecting."

"But Katie, isn't that a bit silly? Shouldn't Hannah just send them over here for their sweet treats?"

"I suppose she could, but Mr. Dell specifically told her to buy some sweets to have in the shop—so that is what she is doing."

"Well, that is what she should do then, I

guess." Frieda looked around. "Hey, where's Mrs. Simpkins? I thought she was coming in early today?"

"She left a note, saying she was busy this morning and wouldn't be in until later." Katie tried not to look worried, so Freida wouldn't suspect anything was wrong.

This morning, after Hannah left, Katie had checked to see if the paper bag was still in the closet. There had been three bottles in the bag on Saturday evening. Today there were two bottles . . . one bottle was missing.

Katie turned to clean up the mess of batter that was covering the already messy workstation.

"*Nee*, Katie, let me do this. You already have to start over. I can clean up this mess and you can go back to work on the batter." With that, Freida took the towel out of Katie's hand to wipe up the mess of batter splattered between them.

"*Jah. Allrecht,* Freida. You go ahead and

clean up. I'll start a new batch of batter."

The two *maedels* worked together in silence for nearly an hour, mixing ingredients and preparing treats to bake for the day, before Freida left the *kichlin* to do whatever needed to be done so the bakery could open on time.

* * *

Katie had a lot of extra baking to do for the Coffee Cup, but she knew that it was important to get everything done before their regular customers began coming in to pick up orders—or to place new orders.

Knowing that Freida could handle prepping the customer area, Katie continued to mix ingredients, rotating trays in and out of the oven whenever the timer sounded.

She split her time between the list that Hannah had given her, and the usual early morning pastries they served their own customers. When she checked the list of special orders, she saw that she had missed one.

Ach. Mrs. Mueller will be here before we even unlock the doors. And she doesn't like to wait. She always seems to be in a hurry to get someplace else.

With that in mind, Katie rushed to find the finishing touches they would need for the cake Mrs. Mueller had ordered, giving a quick thanks to *Gott* that she had baked and iced the cake already.

Just then, she heard Freida's voice coming from the other room.

"Katie, I see Mrs. Mueller. She is on her way here. Is her order ready?"

"*Nee*, it is not." Katie knew she sounded a bit short, but thankfully her *freind* did not seem to notice.

"Don't you worry none, I can distract her while you finish up."

"Bless you, Freida."

"Oh, *jah*. For sure, it will be a blessing if I can manage it." Freida turned back to the customer area with a smile.

Katie could not help but laugh at her *freind's* words. Freida had it exactly right. Mrs. Mueller would not be easily delayed. She had a very strict schedule that she kept—and she expected everyone to comply.

Katie lined her tools up, tucked the instructions into the clip above her decorating table and went to work as quickly as possible, immensely grateful when she saw how simple the instructions were.

Just when the clock in Mrs. Simpkins' office sounded the hour, Katie heard the bell over the front door clang as Freida unlocked and then opened it, admitting their most persistent and punctual customer.

While she decorated, carefully spelling words with the thin line of frosting, Katie could vaguely hear Freida as she greeted Mrs. Mueller and mentioned the weather.

It was a surprise indeed that her attempt at distraction was working, but Katie did not question the blessing—she just went with it, doing everything she could to hurry . . . while not rushing the design.

Katie double-checked her spelling just as she heard Mrs. Mueller inquire about her cake. A moment later, Freida poked her head into the *kichlin* and gave Katie a quizzical expression.

"*Jah*, it's done. Give me a moment to box it up. *Danki*, Freida."

Her only answer was another smile as Freida disappeared toward the front of the store again.

Katie wasted no time settling the cake carefully back in the special order box it had sat in through the night, leaving the flap on the end open so that Mrs. Mueller could easily inspect it without destroying the design.

Katie nearly stumbled when she heard Mrs. Mueller ask Freida about the store window. "Who did you get to paint the beautiful scenes on the front window?"

Freida looked over at Katie as she rounded the corner, clearly uncertain of what to say. Katie did her best to distract Mrs. Mueller with the cake while she decided how to answer in the best possible way.

But Katie didn't have to worry about how best to answer. Mrs. Mueller figured it out for herself after just one look at the cake Katie set down on the counter between them.

"Katie, you painted the window scenes, didn't you dear?"

"Yes, Mrs. Mueller, I did."

"You did a fine job, dear. It's wonderful. Mrs. Simpkins is blessed to have you working for her."

Katie felt a blush spreading across her cheeks and neck at the praise—and all she could do in return was nod.

"You tell Mrs. Simpkins what I said now, you hear?

"Yes, ma'am. I'll let her know"

After choosing several loaves of bread, including two pumpkin and two zucchini, Mrs. Mueller left.

Freida continued to wait on customers, and Katie returned to the *kichlin*.

On the Sixth Day of Christmas . . .

Gingerbread Cookies

Ingredients:
- 1/2 cup butter
- 1/2 cup sugar
- 1/2 cup brown sugar
- 1/4 cup molasses
- 1 large egg
- 2 cups flour
- 1/2 teaspoon ground cinnamon
- 2 teaspoon ground ginger
- ¼ teaspoon ground cloves

Instructions:
1. Cream butter and brown sugar together
2. Stir in molasses, then egg
3. In separate bowl, mix flour with spices
4. Stir in butter/sugar mix
5. If mixture is too moist, add 1 tbsp *or more* flour
6. Knead dough lightly, then chill for 40 minutes

7. Shape dough using cookie cutter of your choice.
8. Bake at 350° for 10-12 minutes

SEVEN

Mrs. Mueller was not the only person to corner Katie throughout the day about her artistic efforts. Nearly every customer who came into the Sweet Shop asked who was responsible for the exceptional . . . beautiful . . . amazing window scenes.

It was mid-morning before the Sweet Shop emptied of customers . . . temporarily, at least.

"*Ach*, it has been a *verrickt* morning." Katie let out a breath as she dropped into one of the chairs in the customer area.

"Perhaps the craziest—and busiest—day I can remember since I began working here." Freida let out a laugh as she swept up a few crumbs from the free samples passed out to customers. "For sure and for certain, mostly because of that." She swept a hand toward the front window.

"*Jah*, and I had no idea it would draw such attention. How do you suppose everyone seems to know it was me who did it?" Katie wiped down the table in front of her, then stood and moved to the next table, carefully wiping it down.

"Would you still have drawn it if you had known? I would have been too *naerfich* to do something so bold, especially if everyone knew I did it. What will your *mamm* and *dat* say? And the Bishop. . ." Freida stopped for a moment and leaned on the broom handle, looking intensely at Katie as she did.

Katie started to answer her *freind*, but realized that she was not certain of the answer.

"I. . . I don't know."

Freida nodded and went back to sweeping, but Katie stood there, thinking about her *freind's* question—and her own answer.

Would I still have drawn it? Did I draw it to get attention? Ach, what would Dat say?

Would Dat tell her she was being prideful and insist that she remove the scenes from the window?

"Katie, I know what you are thinking." Freida interrupted her thoughts. Katie realized she had been slowly wiping in the same circle over and over.

Deliberately, she moved to the next table before answering her *freind*. "And what am I thinking, Freida?"

"You are thinking the window scenes were not a *gut* idea. But you know, 'tis not all that different from the paintings Ida May makes and sells to the *Englischers* that come through town. Besides which, Mrs. Simpkins asked if you could do some Christmas decorating in the shop. It is not as if you drew it for yourself, *jah*?"

Freida's words made sense—and she had the right of it.

"Am I making too much of it?"

Freida spoke again before Katie could say more. "Yes, you are for certain making too much of it, Katie."

"That is sweet of you to say, Freida, but how do I know that to be true?"

"Simple. Because you usually stay in the *kichlin* as much as you can when we have customers. If you are not here to receive their praise, you know it is not about *hochmut*."

Katie thought about that for a moment. Did it make sense? Freida's logic did make sense. Could it really be so simple?

"Katie . . . is *gut* logic, *jah*?"

"*Jah*, Freida, it is a *wunderbaar gut* logic.

And that is just what I will do." And since she had wiped down the last table, Katie went off to the *kichlin* with a smile.

She felt like baking.

Only three customers came into the Sweet Shop over the next two hours, but Katie remained in the *kichlin*, so she couldn't hear well enough to know whether they made a comment on her window art—or not.

She found herself singing quietly to herself as she moved around the *kichlin*, mixing up the usual treats. She even had time to get a head start on some of the orders their customers would be picking up over the following week as they prepared for the coming holidays.

It was nearly eleven when Freida opened the *kichlin* door and popped her head through the opening.

"Katie, Mr. O'Neal is here and he brought us lunch."

"Did we order lunch today?" Katie asked,

even though she knew the answer was no. After all, *Mamm* had packed a plentiful lunch for her and Freida—probably enough for both girls to have lunch again the next day, as well.

"He says he needs our help with something."

"Both of us?"

"*Jah*, both of us."

Her curiosity piqued, Katie covered the dough she was working on and moved over to the sink to wash her hands.

Then she followed Freida out to the customer area, where Andrew O'Neal sat at one of their larger tables, surrounded by sandwiches, bags of assorted chips, soft drinks and several deserts Katie recognized as their own.

She looked over at Freida, who shrugged and walked over to the table, pulled out a chair to sit down and looked back expectantly at Katie.

"Katie, the window design, tis yours, aye?"

Much too curious to be so easily distracted, Katie only nodded, as she moved over to the table and slowly sat down in the third chair.

"An exceptional job that. Well done, Katie."

Katie was determined not to be swayed by Mr. O'Neal's flattery, well aware of his typical tactics by now. He wanted something—she was certain of it. All she could do now was figure out what.

"*Danki*, Mr. O'Neal. What is this help you need from us?"

"Katie, don't you think you should at least say *danki* to Mr. O'Neal for this *wunderbaar* meal before you start interrogating him?"

"Nae, Freida, it's all right. Katie knows me only too well." He laughed before going on. "Yes, dear friend. I am in need of your help. And quickly, before time runs out."

"I thought as much." Katie selected a sandwich and placed it on her plate, along with some chips and one of her favorite treats." After taking a bite, she turned her attention to Andrew. "Now, what is this all about?"

"Ladies, I need help with selecting a gift for a "special" friend. I've thought about it for a while, thinking I could come up with something special, but Christmas is just a few days away—and I still have no idea of what to give this person.

Katie and Freida both looked surprised—even shocked—at what Mr. O'Neal had said. Katie found her voice.

"Are you kidding me! It's five days till Christmas and you haven't bought her a present yet!"

"I know that! Don't you think I know that?" Mr. O'Neal looked flustered for once. "I tell you, I have tried. I've went to more shops than I can care to think about . . . I've looked in catalogs and on the Internet. Nothing . . . there's nothing suitable for someone special; at least, nothing I could give her."

"You've really tried? Honestly?"

"Yes, I've really tried. Nothing seems good enough—or special enough—for such a special lady."

Freida looked thoughtful. "How about stationery or—" she broke off for a moment. "Hey, I know. What are some of her hobbies? You could buy her some knitting needles . . . or yarn . . . or pattern books . . . or quilting squares. Well, you could—if you knew what her hobbies are."

"I have no idea what her hobbies are—or if she has any. It's proved difficult just to get her to talk to me, except on a few rare occasions."

"Let me see what I can find out today and tomorrow. But Mr. O'Neal, you don't have much time left." Katie took another bite of her sandwich. "Why don't we meet back here tomorrow—same time—and I'll share whatever I've learned. But no matter, we'll have to figure something out, or it'll be too late."

Mr. O'Neal looked delighted at the turn of events. "Aye, that is a great idea. I'll be back tomorrow—with lunch."

A moment later he added, with a grin, "And both of you can just stop this nonsense, calling me Mr. O'Neal. I'm Andrew—and ya both know it."

On the Seventh Day of Christmas . . .

Holiday Snickerdoodles

Ingredients:
- 1 cup shortening
- 2 eggs
- 1 ½ cup sugar
- 2 ¾ cup flour
- 2 teaspoon cream of tartar
- 1 teaspoon soda
- 2 tablespoons colored sugar sprinkles
- 1 teaspoon cinnamon

Instructions:
1. Mix together each colored sugar sprinkles and cinnamon
2. Set aside for later
3. Cream together shortening, eggs and sugar
4. Add flour, cream of tartar and baking soda
5. Roll mixture into 1-inch to 2-inch balls *(depending on what size cookie you want)*

6. Roll each ball in a mixture of colored sugar sprinkles and cinnamon
7. Bake at 350° for 10-12 minutes

EIGHT

Soon after their impromptu lunch was over, Mrs. Simpkins came in the back door of the bakery, bringing several bags with her. Katie noticed that she quickly stashed them in the closet—the same closet where Katie had found the paper bag that held three bottles of alcohol.

When Mrs. Simpkins closed the closet door, Katie thought her boss looked a bit flustered, but otherwise seemed fine. She asked how many new orders had been placed, and if customers were picking up the orders as expected.

Katie and Freida assured her that everything was going well, and that there were a great many more orders placed than expected, even for this time of the year.

Freida also told her that everyone who had come into the bakery today had mentioned the beautiful, holiday scenes painted on the window—and how much pleasure it was bringing to everyone.

When she could finally get a word in, Katie asked Mrs. Simpkins if she could leave early, to run an errand.

Mrs. Simpkins gave her permission, so an hour before closing, Katie grabbed the basket with the lunch she had brought to work.

Since Mr. O'Neal had brought their lunch today—and promised lunch again tomorrow, Katie decided to take the food to the Davis family.

* * *

Katie set down the basket her *mamm* had

packed on the weathered, wood porch as she waited for someone to answer her knock.

She looked around at the changes to everything; the house, the yard and the porch she stood on. Since her first visit to this little house, much work had been done.

The boards under her feet had been replaced, re-sanded and repainted. The outer walls of the house had been sanded down and painted as well—and that alone gave the home a much-needed lift.

She knew her *bruders* had helped some of the other youth from her community to do the repairs. Her *mamm* and their neighbors had pitched in to cook for the volunteers—and since Katie had been helping with that, she had not been to visit the Davis family recently—not since everything had been done.

When the front door opened, it did not stick, and the young *maedel* who answered looked almost like a different person than the one Katie had met in July.

"Oh, Katie. Hi." Gwen was already pulling Katie inside; which forced Katie to interrupt her new *freind* so that she could turn and retrieve her basket.

"Wait, Gwen. I need that basket." She stepped back outside and lifted the basket from the porch where she had set it.

"Katie, it is so good to see you!" And she rushed forward to envelop her in a hug.

"But you didn't have to bring us anything. Your family has done so much for us already."

Katie waved away the *maedel's* objection. "Now, don't you tell me those *bruders* of yours will not enjoy this. Why, if they eat anywhere near as much as mine, this will disappear in no time."

"Well, you're right about how much those boys eat. But they haven't exactly been starving lately." She laughed a little as she said it and turned to head in the direction

CHRISTMAS COOKIE MYSTERY

Katie remembered seeing the *kichlin*.

The change in Gwen was a relief to Katie. It was so *gut* to hear the young *maedel* laugh.

She was so quiet and shy when I first met her. For sure and for certain this time has done her plenty of gut.

Katie followed Gwen into the *kichlin* and was surprised to see the counters were nearly full of plates and platters filled with treats that looked simply *appeditlich*.

There were cookies, pies, home-made breads, and a large plate covered with what looked like slices of several different types of cheese.

That one must have been from one of our Englischer neighbors.

She saw several casserole dishes; some of them were full and covered with foil or plastic wrap, while others were empty, but those were washed, and stacked neatly with other clean dishes. There was also nearly half of a ham sitting on the counter. It was still wrapped, but there was a fog under the plastic; as if someone had just taken it out of the refrigerator.

"*Jah*, I see what you mean."

Gwen turned with a mischievous smile on her face. "Between your neighbors and ours, we have certainly not been starving lately." She laughed again and this time Katie joined her. With all that she had been worrying over lately, it was *gut* to laugh.

Katie found that she felt less burdened when she and Gwen finally began to calm their laughter.

"Well, now I don't know what to do with this lunch that *Mamm* packed."

"I am more than happy to take it. Even with all of this, it will not go to waste. I can promise you that."

"If you are sure." Katie would certainly not want the *wunderbaar* meal *Mamm* had packed up to miss out on being enjoyed. And she did not feel even a little bothered by the idea of sharing with the Davis family. *Mamm* had packed the lunch to be shared—and shared it most certainly would be.

"It will be a welcome addition to lunch. We have so many sweets, but hardly anyone thinks to bring more than that. I have made the boys eat ham for the last three meals just so they get something other than treats."

"I should warn you, there is a pie in here, too." Katie laughed again as she said it—and after a second, so did Gwen.

"Well, your mom knows how to pack a well-balanced lunch."

"Of course."

They both laughed again as Gwen opened the large basket and started pulling things out.

Katie watched as the spread of items grew. Every time she was certain it must be the last thing, Gwen would pull another out.

"My goodness, this just may feed us for two meals."

"*Jah*, I think that was *Mamm's* intention."

"Well, she nailed it. Wow! This is a lot of food."

"*Jah*, it certainly is. *Mamm* must have been thinking I would bring the extras here. You don't have to take everything out, you know." Katie teased her.

"I know I don't. I just figured this way, you can take the basket back with you. You won't have to wait for us to finish everything."

"*Jah*, that is *gut* thinking, Gwen. *Danki*." After a second, she added, "Of course, it's not like I won't be seeing you in the next few days."

"Or Travis, at least."

Gwen spoke without looking up and Katie nearly asked her where he was working today, but stopped herself just before the words left her mouth.

It would not do to give her the wrong idea.

On the Eighth Day of Christmas . . .

Christmas Fudge
Kid Friendly Recipe

Ingredients:

    2 cups peanut butter

    2 cups confectioner's sugar

    2 tablespoons butter, melted

    1/2 tablespoon pure vanilla extract

    1/2 tablespoon pure almond extract

Instructions:

1. Line a square baking pan with wax paper *(8x8 works best)*
2. Mix ingredients together
3. Spread out on the baking pan
4. Refrigerate for 1 hour *(or until hard)*
5. Cut into small squares
6. Enjoy

** For extra flavor, add 1/2 cup semi sweet chocolate chips, just before time to spread mixture out in the baking pan.

NINE

Katie walked into the barn after Ervin, her big *bruder*. As she glanced around, looking for Freida, she wandered over to the large, pot-bellied cook stove where Maddie Mae Zook was stirring a large crock of what Katie really hoped was hot cocoa.

She had not made it into the barn without first being pelted with snowballs. The *buwes* had been deep into a snow battle when she arrived, and she had walked right into it, before she had realized why it was so quiet outside the barn.

"Katie!" Hannah had appeared beside Maddie Mae with a thick mug she must have brought with her, waving a hand to Katie.

The two were deep in discussion when Katie walked up. Almost immediately, Maddie Mae placed a mug of cocoa in Katie's hands. She stood there, holding it between her gloved hands, just letting the warmth soak into her cold fingers, while she listened to the two girls chatting.

"Oh, *nee*. I could never drink *kaffe* so late in the day. I would never get to sleep. It's difficult enough with the cocoa. That is why I usually volunteer to stir. I can breathe the *wunderbaar* smell and I get to be right here by the fire all evening, so I don't need to drink any of it to stay warm."

With an unsuspecting smile, Hannah answered back, "*Jah*, but how will you ever know if one of the Yoder *buwes* shines a flashlight in your window if you just go to sleep each night?"

Maddie Mae cuffed Hannah playfully on the arm then. "*Ach*, Hannah you are too much." Both of them were laughing when Katie joined them.

"Katie, I am so glad you are here." Hannah leaned in to give her *freind* a hug, before going on. "I was worried you might still be working at the bakery. The lights were on when John Baker picked me up to bring me home."

Katie was certain she knew who had been at the bakery, but she did not say anything to Hannah or Maddie Mae, lest word get around about Mrs. Simpkins. Instead, she stuck to as much of the truth as she could without raising suspicions.

"It is quite busy this time of year, you know."

"Don't I know it! All I have to do at the Coffee Cup is make *kaffe* and serve the treats. You have to make all of the treats." She laid a hand on Katie's arm before going on.

"By the way, *danki* for helping me out with those treats. Even though the delivery finally showed up this morning, Mr. Dell wants to talk to Mrs. Simpkins about a standing order for several types of pastries from the bakery. This would also ensure that everything is fresher, too."

"They sold well, then?" Katie asked, trying to keep her words from sounding too excited.

"They certainly did." She waved a hand at Katie before going on. "We definitely noticed a difference in the sales from Monday and yesterday—and the sales for today, too."

"Could that just be the holiday season, though?"

"*Nee*, I don't think so. The supplier Mr. Dell orders the pastries from now does not carry anything like those *wunderbaar* chocolate croissants you brought me—and even the regular croissants you sent over sold much faster than what we have been getting. Yours simply look more *appeditlich*. Mr. Dell said since the contract with the supplier is ending in a few days, it's the best time to change suppliers."

Maddie Mae spoke up before Katie could respond. "Ooh, that is exciting, Katie."

"It is exciting. I am certain Mrs. Simpkins will be pleased to hear it." Katie hoped some *gut* news would help the dear lady to cheer up.

Of course, she was also hoping Mr. O'Neal's gift—if he could find one in time—would help. Beyond that, she was still unsure of how to even approach her usually sensible boss.

"Katie, look, they are lining up to start the singing." Maddie Mae rushed off to get in line with the other young people.

Katie stayed where she was, hoping the warmth from the stove would chase away the chill from her bones.

It was only a minute before the group began singing one of Katie's favorite hymns. She did not join in from where she stood, but she could feel a warmth spreading through her as she listened to her neighbors' voices raised in song.

"Wow! They're really good."

Katie jumped; startled at the all-too-familiar voice.

Ach, what is he doing here? She forced herself to take several breaths before turning to greet the only person here who could make her go weak in the knees.

"They are not singing to be *gut*, but I know what you mean. There is very little in this world that is as wondrous as a group of people with their voices raised in song to praise *Gott*."

"It's too bad they don't sing to be *gut*. They would really make a fantastic choir."

Katie looked up quickly at his use of

her Dietsch word, but was quickly distracted by the remainder of his sentence.

"Why would they want to be a choir? What would be the use or purpose of that, if not to do just what they are doing now?"

"All I mean is that it's a shame more people don't get to enjoy such beautiful music. The world could use more of such pure praise."

She wanted to answer back—to somehow make him understand—but could think of no answer that would properly explain, so she kept quiet and thought over his statement.

"I'm sorry. Really Katie, I meant no harm. Christmas is one of those times I get especially sentimental and it really bothers me to see how the world is wrecking things . . . especially Christmas."

She looked up at him then, surprised to hear such passion over something so simple as hymns.

Or perhaps it is not so simple, after all.

Suddenly, she had an idea about the dear, sweet lady she had worked for over a year now. "Travis, do you think that could be the same thing that might be what is bothering Mrs. Simpkins?"

He looked at her for a moment, before understanding lit in his expression. "You could be on to something there. The real question is—what could we possibly do about it?"

That stopped Katie from answering. "That, I do not know. But we can pray about it."

"That sounds like an idea."

"*Jah*, we can certainly pray about it. And I will mention it to *Mamm* as well."

"You're not going to. . ."

Katie interrupted before he could finish that thought. "*Nee*. That is not what I meant."

"Whew." Travis let out a heavy breath then. "You had me worried for a second there."

"I am only going to ask her about ideas for cheering up Mrs. Simpkins."

"But don't you think that will cause her to ask how you know Mrs. Simpkins needs cheering up?"

Katie started to speak, but the words turned into a "hmm" when she closed her mouth again.

After a moment she added, "You have a point. I didn't think of that. Well, what do you suggest?"

"I don't know. I just know it would be a bad idea to say too much to anyone before we know what's really going on."

"*Jah.* I agree."

The two of them stood there for several minutes, listening to the singing. The group had finished one song and started another, when Maddie Mae appeared next to Katie and stirred the enormous crock of hot cocoa.

* * *

After Maddie Mae appeared, Travis quickly headed in the direction of the Yoder brothers. For one thing, he didn't want anyone questioning why he was hanging around Katie. For another, he really did need to talk to them.

When he reached them, they were in a lively discussion about the Second Christmas dinner they were looking forward to.

Timothy was the first to speak to him. "Hey, Trav. Glad you could make it. Are you getting along okay so far? Have you met many of the others here?"

"Not everyone, but yeah, a few people. I think some of them are a bit nervous around me."

"*Jah*, not many *Englischers* join us at the singings. But if you're gonna be working with some of these *buwes*, I thought this would be the best chance to get to know them."

"That's a great idea."

"All right, then. Let's go meet everyone you don't know. Just don't you go and ask any of the *maedel's* if you can give them a ride home tonight." And with a wink, Timothy motioned for his *bruder* to join them.

When they reached the barn, they were all laughing over one of Tim's tall tales.

On the Ninth Day of Christmas . . .

Salted Caramel Peanut Butter Cookies

Ingredients:

    24 vanilla caramels

    1/2 cup butter, softened

    3/4 cup creamy peanut butter

    1/3 cup sugar

    1/3 cup light brown sugar, packed

    1 large egg

    2 tablespoons milk

    1 teaspoon pure vanilla extract

    1-1/2 cups all-purpose flour

    1 teaspoon baking soda

    1/2 teaspoon salt

    Ground sea salt

Instructions:

    1. Preheat oven to 350°

    2. Using hot knife, cut caramels in half

    3. Mix butter and peanut butter until well blended

    4. Add sugars; beat until fluffy

5. Add egg, milk and vanilla; mix well
6. Stir together flour, baking soda and salt
7. Gradually add flour mixture, mixing thoroughly
8. Refrigerate for at least 1 hour
9. Shape dough into 1-inch balls
10. Bake 8-10 minutes or until lightly browned
11. Immediately press a caramel piece into center of each cookie
12. Sprinkle with sea salt
13. Return to oven for 1-2 minutes
14. Remove from cookie sheet to wire rack
15. Cool completely

TEN

Katie watched through the side window of the bakery at the town square while she wiped down tables in the customer area.

One by one, children were making their way to the Santa who sat in the midst of an elaborately decorated North Pole. For the past few weeks, the *North Pole* had taken over the park that usually occupied the center of town.

From here it was impossible to tell who was who, but there was something about the crowd . . . a joy that simply glowed—from the long line of excited children—to their happy parents.

While their customers—including Mrs. Mueller and three of her neighbors, who came in every day to enjoy the Sweet Shop's treats. . . and a bit of gossip—spoke in hushed tones behind her, Katie slowly wiped down each table, and watched as each child took their turn to sit on Santa's lap.

Even though every visit was essentially the same, she could spot little differences in each one.

One child reached up to whisper into Santa's ear, while another was clearly pronouncing their wish loudly enough for even those in the back of the line to hear—judging from what sounded like delighted laughter from the parents . . . and Santa's helpers.

As the line rounded a curve, a child she would recognize anywhere came into sight. She moved closer to the window to be certain, but her improved view only confirmed what she had already known; the child was little Bobby Davis, and if she wasn't mistaken, the person who held his hand—while he bounced as high as a kangaroo—was his big *bruder*, Travis.

She watched as they moved slowly forward in the line—the tables forgotten for the moment—watching Bobby skip forward each time they moved and then, when they stood still, the bouncing resumed.

At one point, Bobby must have caught sight of Santa because she was certain he bounced higher than Travis' head for a moment. When he touched back down, he jumped closer to his *bruder* and shouted something. She couldn't tell what it was, but it must have been loud, because several parents around them in line turned to smile at the young boy and his big *bruder*.

"Katie, where are you. . . Oh, there you are." Freida's voice startled Katie, and she reluctantly turned from the window.

"What is it, Freida?"

"I just wanted to remind you that Mr. Mentink is going to be here in a few minutes to pick up the other half of today's order . . ." She looked around the customer area and then leaned in to whisper behind her hand to Katie. "The one for Santa."

Katie wanted to laugh, but she restrained herself. One time . . .

Freida had announced the same message last year when the town treasurer had been on his way over to pick up the afternoon portion of their daily cookie order for Santa's helpers.

The Sweet Shop had been full of children and there had evidently been a few awkward questions from one of their more precocious customers.

Katie had been in the *kichlin* at the time and apparently Freida had said something wrong, because Katie remembered hearing a scream and the voices of several children raised in argument before Freida had burst through the *kichlin* door, her face white as a sheet.

Katie had dusted off her hands and rushed out front as quickly as possible. The children's parents had already managed to calm them down, but Freida had refused to set foot outside the *kichlin* until after Christmas.

"Bradley Post still sticks his tongue out at me every time he sees me."

"Bradley Post is seven, Freida."

"I know that. And it isn't as if I really ruined anyone's Christmas, but—"

"I know." Katie patted her *freind* on the shoulder as she handed over the wet cloth and turned to go behind the counter, taking one last look at the line of children as she did so.

They had made their way to the front and little Bobby was running over to Santa, practically throwing himself in the jolly man's lap—while Travis stood at the front of the line waiting for his *bruder*.

Even from so far away, Katie could see the worry etched into Travis' face. It took no more than a moment to realize what he was worried over.

Mrs. Simpkins paid him enough to pay the mortgage on their house and the other monthly bills they had, but Katie doubted there was enough left over to do much more than buy groceries for the family.

And even though the entire town had practically adopted the little family, bringing them food nearly every day, Katie knew that would not help Travis to feel less guilty about having no money to buy Christmas gifts for his *bruders* and *schweschder*.

Here I have been worrying over finding time to finish the gifts for my own family—and Travis likely has nothing to give to his mother, or his *bruders* and *schweschder*.

Katie tried to think of something she could do, but it was two days till Christmas and would likely be too late at this point.

Ach! Why did I not think of this earlier?

She tried reminding herself that it was not exactly something that had *kumme* up between the two of them while they were working. And it was also a bit personal. It wasn't as if she'd had a *gut* reason to just ask him what he was buying everyone for Christmas.

But the worry settled in her stomach like a rock, piling on top of the worry over getting her own gifts finished . . . and getting everything done at the bakery.

Then she realized there was one who could do so much more than she ever could—one she could go to about it.

Dear Gott, only you have the power to help with this. There is no time for me to do anything about it and I know Travis cannot or he would not be worrying over it now.

NAOMI MILLER

Please provide for this precious family, dear Gott.

On the Tenth Day of Christmas . . .

Festive Sugar Cookies

Ingredients:
- 1 cup butter, softened
- 1 1/2 cups sugar
- 2 large eggs
- 1 teaspoon pure vanilla extract
- 1 teaspoon pure almond extract
- 2 1/2 cups plain flour
- 1/2 teaspoon baking powder
- 1/2 teaspoon salt

Instructions:
1. Preheat oven to 350°
2. Line cookie sheets with parchment paper
3. Cream together butter and sugar until light and fluffy, about 3 minutes
4. Add egg and mix until well-combined
5. Stir in flour, baking powder, salt, and vanilla
6. Scoop cookie dough by the tablespoon full and roll into a ball

7. Place cookie dough onto baking sheet, spacing about 1½-inches to 2 inches apart
8. Lightly press each cookie down
9. Bake for 8-10 minutes or until lightly browned

Note: When cookies are cool, feel free to decorate—or not.

If you add frosting, set cookies aside to allow it to dry completely. Store in tightly covered container (wax paper between layers) up to 2 weeks.

ELEVEN

Friday began with light flurries, with the promise of a white Christmas for the inhabitants of Abbott Creek.

Katie rushed around the *kichlin*, working feverishly to make certain every last order was ready for pickup. They were only open until eleven and they were opening a half hour early to accommodate all of the customers who were picking up orders for Christmas.

"Katie, are we ready? Freida will be

opening the door in five minutes."

Even amidst the stress and worry of Christmas Eve, there was a great deal of relief within Katie for how different Amelia Simpkins sounded this morning.

She was positively radiant with excitement—and Katie was certain it was entirely natural, which made her feel a lot better about their plan for the small party they would have just after closing today, before everyone went their separate ways to celebrate Christmas.

"I believe so, Mrs. Simpkins." She took a deep breath, then another look at the list in her hand, before adding, "*Jah*, we are ready."

Amelia nodded, and then turned to move through the kitchen door.

* * *

Earlier, Mrs. Simpkins had confided in her that she had been staying late, night after night, trying to re-create a recipe for cookies that Mr. O'Neal's grandmother had made for him.

She had tried using Irish Whiskey in the recipe, but finally decided to try a substitute. She had given Andrew the cookies last night, and he had been delighted with them!

Katie was relieved to finally know the mystery had been solved—that the bottles she had found in the closet had been for a *gut* purpose.

Mrs. Simpkins had also confided that Mr. O'Neal had presented her with a special gift—an heirloom brooch that had belonged to his grandmother, then passed on to his own mother, before he gave it to Amelia.

Danki, dear Lord. Two very dear people have each received a blessing—for sure and for certain—and will have a wunderbaar gut Christmas.

And I am certain the Davis children will not go unnoticed by their *freinden* in the community. I know you will be working this out in a *wunderbaar* way.

* * *

Less than a minute later, Katie heard the sound of many feet on linoleum as the customers, who had been lined up and waiting outside, gathered inside the Sweet Shop.

It was only a few seconds later that Mrs. Simpkins walked into the kitchen and gave Katie the first of many names.

Katie wasted no time in moving into the walk-in cooler for the box of treats for Mrs. Mueller, smiling at the thought that she was not in the least surprised at who had commanded the first place in line.

She was likely up with the cows to get here so early.

Katie passed the box to her boss and then checked the name off her list. She had no more than set the pencil down, when Freida moved through the *kichlin* door with the next order.

* * *

CHRISTMAS COOKIE MYSTERY

The morning moved quickly after that. Never once did the steady stream of customers let up—and no one lost their temper or showed impatience.

Only once did Katie hear raised voices—and when the *kichlin* door opened, she could hear music, and soon realized that it was several people out front, who had decided to entertain those waiting in line, with Christmas carols.

When Freida walked into the *kichlin* for the next order, she propped the door open so that Katie could enjoy the impromptu concert as well.

Mrs. Simpkins practically sang out the next order name when she came in a minute later—and Katie laughed when she realized her boss was humming the same song the carolers were singing as she went back out to deliver the order.

* * *

Travis opened the back door to the

bakery and smiled at the sight that greeted him. Katie was singing quietly as she moved between the counter top and the wall where her list hung.

Mrs. Simpkins and Freida were moving back and forth, between the *kichlin* and the customer area, both humming along to the same song.

And there was the sweet sound of his favorite Christmas carols wafting in through the open *kichlin* door.

He stood there for several minutes, watching the scene before him as it repeated —almost as if it were a movie on some sort of loop. . . except for the song changing after several minutes.

His observation was broken when Katie noticed him standing just inside the door.

"Oh *gut*! You are here just in time." She clapped her hands together before adding, "We have several orders that must go out this morning."

"Are any of them in need of delicate handling?" He asked with a grin, remembering the first delicate order Katie had sent him out with. "It is a blessing you are so talented with your decorating. I would never have been able to salvage that mess."

He laughed when Katie swatted him playfully.

"Yes, as a matter of fact, the Mayor's order requires delicate handling, but I am sending it with you first. . . and all by itself."

"So you have time to fix it if I mess it up?"

"Travis Davis, you had best not mess it up. I will never be able to fix it if you do." She swatted him again before he held up both hands in surrender.

"Hey, hey . . . I'm only joking. I will be extremely careful. I promise."

"*Gut,* because this is the main attraction for the Mayor's Christmas table and he will not be pleased if it is ruined."

"I believe you."

"*Gut*." Katie nodded solemnly before turning toward the oversized walk-in cooler.

It was nearly a minute before she returned, carrying an enormous box that must have been specially made for this "fragile" desert the mayor had ordered.

She carefully slid it onto a rolling cart that was waiting right outside the cooler door. Travis moved over to help her roll it carefully across the *kichlin*, pushing against the *kichlin* door and then lifting with her as they moved over the threshold.

Once outside, they eased the cart down again and slowly rolled it down the gradual ramp that switched back and forth along the back of the building beside a short flight of steps.

"This thing looks really fancy. I didn't think the plain folk approved of such fancy things." Travis meant for the comment to sound genuine, but apparently Katie took it as teasing, because she answered with more than a little snap in her voice.

"We don't approve of owning fancy things, but we don't mind making them for *Englischers* who want them."

"Katie, I've seen your quilts. I know just how crazy talented your family is. I was trying to pay you a compliment. You were in such a great mood when I got here and now I've ruined it. I'm really sorry."

"No, I am the one who is sorry, Travis. You are right. It is not really that. Truly, I did not mean to snap at you."

"Did you get the presents done?"

"*Jah*, I did."

"And the customer pickups are going well?"

"Oh, *jah*. For sure and for certain they are."

"Then what's the problem? Is it me?"

Katie looked down at the ground as they maneuvered the cart gently over the uneven ground between the end of the ramp and the delivery van's back doors, which Travis had opened before coming inside.

"Katie, what is it?" When she didn't answer again, he added, "Is it me? You can tell me."

She let out a long breath before answering. "*Nee*, it is not really you. It is just . . . many things. Please forgive me?"

"Of course. I know how stressful this time of year can be."

It might have been his imagination, but he thought she looked even more stressed than before they talked.

* * *

When Travis left with the special desert for the mayor, Katie watched the van until it disappeared around the corner. Then she closed her eyes and bowed her head once more.

Dear Gott, please help me to have peace about this. I have asked for your help, with my feelings for Travis, and with his family not having Christmas gifts. There is nothing more I can do now. Please help me to know everything is going to be okay."

A sense of peace settled over Katie —just as the first rays of sunlight broke through the horizon and the sky filled with the most amazing colors.

And she knew. . . *Gott* had something in motion already.

* * *

When Mrs. Simpkins walked into the *kichlin* a moment later, Katie waited for her to call out a customer's name.

"Katie, there are some people out front, who want to speak with you." Mrs. Simpkins looked a bit *naerfich*. She waited for Katie to pass, then followed her through the doorway.

Katie's *dat* was waiting for her, along with Preacher Amos. Neither of them looked very *froh*—happy—right now.

"Katie, am I to understand that you were

the one who painted all the pictures on the window over there?"

"*Jah*, Amos. That was me, for sure."

"And did you seek council from your *dat* or the Bishop, before doing so?"

"*Nee*. I thought perhaps it would be considered part of my *rumschpringe*."

"She has a point there, Amos." Katie's *dat* spoke up.

"*Jah*, Caleb. That is something to think on, for sure." Preacher Amos turned from Katie's *dat*—to the window—and back to her for a moment. "Katie, I think we can perhaps overlook this wrongdoing—this one time."

"*Danki*, Amos."

"Sir, I want to assure you—to assure you both—that Katie has not even been talking to the customers about her artwork. She has been staying in the kitchen to work this week." Mrs. Simpkins looked over at Katie, giving her a smile, then turned back to the man who had been doing most of the talking.

Preacher Amos looked over at Mrs. Simpkins, then back to Katie. When he spoke again, he seemed to be speaking to Mrs. Simpkins.

"*Danki.* We will not be bothering you further. Come along, Caleb. You and I have much to do today, *jah*?" Preacher Amos turned toward the door.

Katie's *dat* smiled at her, tipped his hat to Mrs. Simpkins, then followed Preacher Amos out the door.

As new customers came in, Katie hurried back to the *kichlin* to give herself a moment to catch her breath—before heading back into the cooler to pick up the customer's order.

Hmm. I wonder what Dat and Amos had to do that sounded so urgent. . .

On the Eleventh Day of Christmas . . .

Irish Gingerbread Cookies

Ingredients:
- 3 tablespoons butter
- 3 tablespoons dark brown sugar*
- 3 tablespoons sugar
- 1 large egg yolk
- 1/2 tablespoon pure vanilla extract
- 1/2 tablespoon pure almond extract
- 1/3 cup flour
- 1/3 teaspoon baking powder
- 1/4 teaspoon baking soda
- 1/3 teaspoon ground cinnamon
- 1/8 teaspoon salt
- 1/2 cup quick-cook oats *(I prefer steel cut)*

Instructions:
1. Preheat the oven to 350°
2. Line a cookie sheet with parchment paper
3. Cream together the butter and sugars *(with an electric mixer)*
4. Add egg yolk
5. Mix until combined

CHRISTMAS COOKIE MYSTERY

6. Add vanilla and almond extract and mix
7. Sprinkle the flour, baking powder, baking soda, cinnamon and salt over the mixture
8. Mix until combined
9. Stir in the oats
10. Scoop heaping tablespoons of dough and lightly roll into balls
11. Bake for 10-12 minutes
12. Let cookies cool completely on cookie sheet
13. Makes about 1 dozen cookies
14.

You may store in an air-tight container for up to 3 days

Notes:

The flavor of dark brown sugar really shines in this recipe. If you only have light brown sugar, you can add extra molasses. Per 1 cup of light brown sugar, stir in 1 tablespoon of molasses *(Do not use 1 cup in this recipe. Save the excess for use in a later recipe).*

Also. . . you'll notice we put the recipe Mrs. Simpkins actually used in the book. . . not the one Mr. O'Neal remembers his dear sweet Grandmother making all those years.

Since he cannot actually remember just how much Irish whiskey she put in the recipe, Mrs. Simpkins did a bit of experimenting to come up with this recipe.

Also, since Mrs. Simpkins does not drink, she asked Travis to look up a suitable substitution— which he found online.

──── TWELVE ────

Travis crept downstairs as quietly as possible. He knew Bobby would be up at the slightest of sounds—and what little surprise he had would be ruined.

He had waited up as long as possible last night with everyone, until he finally had to admit that the early morning hours were taking their toll on him. He had consoled himself with the knowledge that he could come down early in the morning to arrange everything under the tree, with little fear that anyone else would be up before him.

Feeling his way along the wall, so that he would not lose his footing, he slipped silently through the hall, heading toward the living room.

Once his eyes adjusted to the tiny amount of light that came from the fire he had banked last night before going up to bed, he realized he wasn't alone in the room.

It was no surprise to find his mother asleep on the couch. She had not said anything to him about wanting to move—and though she was perfectly capable of traversing the hallway by herself now that she was on the mend—he still wished she had at least said something to him, given him a chance to help get her settled, something. . .

A quick, hard rap at the front door had him nearly jumping out of his skin.

He set down the bag he carried as carefully—and as quickly—as possible, and rushed to the door before the person could knock again and risk waking anyone.

Pulling open the door, he expected to see one of his neighbors—or likely one of Katie's—on the porch with sweets or treats for Christmas morning, wanting to deliver them early before they headed out to their visiting.

But there was no one in sight.

After a moment, he stepped over the threshold, crossing his arms over his chest in deference to the cold, and looked around for any sign of who had knocked. He looked left. He looked right.

No one was there.

He looked at the houses on either side and then across the street, wondering if perhaps it had been one of their neighbors, but all of the houses were still dark.

Perplexed, he stepped forward, bare feet and all, and his toe bumped hard against something.

When he looked down to see what he had bumped into, certain it must be some sort of basket filled with food, he saw instead a large pile of brightly wrapped gifts.

His first reaction was that it must be some sort of mistake, but the box on the very top showed a tag peeking out from under an enormous bow that read "Bobby".

When he lifted it from the pile, he found another one underneath, bearing Bobby's name and yet another one with the name "Gwen"—written in a decorative sort of script.

He turned and walked across the porch, from end to end, searching for any sign of who had brought this to them. There was no clue whatsoever, no matter where he searched.

There was nothing.

Four trips later, he managed to bring in the last of the gifts. He immediately went to work getting them settled under the tree. Obviously whoever had done this was determined to play Santa—and Travis had a feeling that he might never know who it had been.

Once he arranged everything to his satisfaction, including enough candy, fruit and nuts to fill all their stockings—socks that each one had contributed for Santa to fill—that had been in bags beside the pile of gifts, he went off to the kitchen to set out breakfast.

We are going to eat breakfast together, as a family, before presents are opened.

While he sorted through pastries, biscuits and bagels that had been dropped off over the last week, he thought of the gifts.

Why would someone do that—just leave them all out there with no hint of where they had come from?

And how did they get away so quickly?

Travis had opened the door within seconds of the knock, but whoever it was had managed to get completely out of sight before the door was opened.

He suddenly realized that he was questioning a miraculous deed, when he should be thanking God that his brothers and sister would have a nice Christmas. With a quick prayer of thanks, he felt happier than he had in a very long time.

* * *

Travis and his mom watched as everyone ripped into the festive paper covering their presents. Each time someone opened something new, the click of his mother's camera sounded beside him.

They watched as Bobby opened a small remote controlled car, a popular building set with hundred of tiny plastic bricks, and a box that held a thick, navy blue coat, a pair of boots and a large pack of socks.

When Travis asked Bobby if he was excited about his gifts, his little brother answered with a wide grin.

"I love it all! And especially the socks!"

"You mean you wanted socks for

Christmas?"

"I did. I asked Santa for them. I always end up with Trevor's socks when he can't fit no more. I wanted some of my very own."

Travis smiled at his enthusiastic baby brother as he thought about his answer. Bobby had asked Santa for socks. That would have to mean it was someone there who heard what he asked for.

Of course, that could be anyone. Half the town was lined up that afternoon, waiting for their turn with the jolly old elf—who just happened to bear a striking resemblance to a certain proprietor I know.

It could even have been Mr. O'Neal himself. Travis thought back to the night he had dropped Katie off and headed home to find Mr. O'Neal and his nephew entertaining everyone in the den.

He could have even used that visit to figure out what everyone else might want for Christmas—since every gift seemed to be the perfect fit for the recipient.

But it could be just as possible that Mr. O'Neal gave the information to someone else, who played Santa for his family. In the meantime, there was no reason to worry about it.

His family was safe, warm, fed, and having a splendid Christmas. The wisest thing to do would be to ask God to bless whoever was responsible, then to relax and enjoy this time with his family.

And that is exactly what he did!

On the Twelfth Day of Christmas . . .

Irish Salted Chocolate Cookies

Cookie Ingredients:
- 1 cup butter, softened
- 1/3 cup sugar
- 1/3 cup brown sugar
- 1 teaspoon pure vanilla extract
- 1 teaspoon pure almond extract
- 2 cups plain flour

Filling Ingredients:
- 11 oz vanilla caramels
- 3 Tablespoons Heavy Whipping Cream
- 1 teaspoon pure vanilla extract
- 1 teaspoon pure almond extract
- Ground Sea Salt

Instructions:
1. Preheat oven to 350°
2. Cream the butter and sugars together

3. Add the vanilla and almond extracts and blend together
4. Slowly add flour, mix
5. Roll dough into 24 balls
6. Place on lined baking sheet.
7. Using a spoon, press down to flatten cookie and make little crater for filling.
8. Bake 10-12 minutes.
9. After removing from oven, use spoon if you desire deeper crater in cookie.
10. Cool cookies on baking sheet for a few minutes.
11. Place cookies, still on lined paper, on a rack to cool.
12. Melt caramels and cream, over medium-low heat, stirring constantly.
13. Remove filling from heat and add vanilla and almond extracts.
14. Fill the crater of each cookie with caramel.

If desired, sprinkle cookies with ground sea salt.

CHRISTMAS COOKIE MYSTERY

Note:

This recipe also called for Irish Whiskey originally, but we substituting vanilla and almond flavoring for it.

And she brought forth her firstborn son, and wrapped him in swaddling clothes, and laid him in a manger; because there was no room for them in the inn.

And there were in the same country shepherds abiding in the field, keeping watch over their flock by night.

And, lo, the angel of the Lord came upon them, and the glory of the Lord shone round about them: and they were sore afraid.

And the angel said unto them, Fear not: for, behold, I bring you good tidings of great joy, which shall be to all people.

For unto you is born this day in the city of David a Saviour, which is Christ the Lord.

And this shall be a sign unto you; Ye shall find the babe wrapped in swaddling clothes, lying in a manger.

And suddenly there was with the angel a multitude of the heavenly host praising God, and saying,

Glory to God in the highest, and on earth peace, good will toward men.

Luke 2:7-14

RECIPE INDEX

Page	Recipe
25	Frosted Christmas Cookies
39	Gingersnap Cookies
52	Irish Shortbread Cookies
61	Pecan Drop Cookies
77	Christmas Date Cookies
89	Gingerbread Cookies
101	Holiday Snickerdoodles
111	Christmas Fudge
124	Salted Caramel Peanut Butter Cookies
135	Festive Sugar Cookies
150	Irish Gingerbread Cookies
161	Irish Salted Chocolate Cookies

TURN THE PAGE

FOR EXCLUSIVE

BONUS CONTENT

DISCUSSION QUESTIONS

WARNING : SPOILERS AHEAD!

1) When you read about Katie on a ladder—using spray paint—what was the first thing that came to mind? Did you feel the same way as Travis . . . that her family and the church elders would not approve of what she was doing?

2) In the same situation as Katie, finding what she found in the paper bag, would you have come to the same conclusion . . . that the contents of the paper bag could lead to trouble? What would you have done in Katie's place?

3) Were you surprised when Travis hugged Katie? Did it seem casual and friendly, or something more?

4) Do you think Travis is right to be concerned about Mr. O'Neal and his mother? Did you pick up any signals from Gwen—and Mr. O'Neal's nephew? Do you think Gwen is old enough to start thinking about boys *in that way*, or should she wait a few more years?

5) Was Katie right to stay in the kitchen, where she couldn't hear what others were saying about her artwork? Do you think the opinions of others should influence you—and the things you do?

6) Who do you think played *Santa Claus* for the Davis family? Have you ever played *Santa* for someone else, especially for someone in need? Has someone ever played *Santa* for you at a time when you were in need?

7) In this world, where so many people work to divide us—as families, friends, or neighbors—do you find it refreshing to read a story where everyone works as a community?

AUTHOR INTERVIEW

Q: What was your inspiration for writing Christmas Cookie Mystery, the second book in the Amish Sweet Shop Mystery series?

A: My inspiration came from Christmas—naturally—but also to write about the good in people, especially around my favorite holiday. Even when people in the book suspect others of doing wrong, they don't jump in and make things worse; instead, they pray and try to think of ways to help.

Q: What do you hope your readers will take away from reading Christmas Cookie Mystery—or others in the series?

A: I hope readers will read this book—this series—and find faith, hope, love, and forgiveness. And I'm hoping to share that the spirit of Christmas can include Santa, who represents the spirit of giving. Santa can be a positive influence in your home.

Q: Will there be more books in the Amish Sweet Shop Mystery series?

A: Oh, yes. I'm working on book three now, titled Lemon Tart Mystery. If all goes well, the fourth book, Pumpkin Pie Mystery, will be released early October 2017.

Q: What does your writing space look like?

A: My writing space is a beautiful desk, left to me by my sister. But, most of the time, I'm either sitting at the dining room table, or sitting on the couch, with my laptop. Honestly, I can write most anywhere, but my favorite place seems to be the dining room table.

Q: What is your favorite Bible verse and why?

A: I have many favorites—too many to list all of them, but I'm happy to share one with you today!

"Trust in the Lord with all thine heart; and lean not unto thine own understanding. In all thy ways acknowledge him, and he shall direct thy paths." ~Proverbs 3:5-6

Q: Do you have a favorite scene in your newest release?

A: Yes! My favorite scene is at the very beginning, when Katie does something totally unexpected—and has a great time doing it!

Q: Where can readers connect with you?

A: Here are the links for each site:

NEWSLETTER SIGN UP: http://eepurl.com/bPdjGn
WEBSITE: https://naomimillerauthor.com
FACEBOOK: www.facebook.com/NaomiMillerAuthor
TWITTER: https://twitter.com/AuthorNaomi
INSTAGRAM: https://twitter.com/AuthorNaomi
PINTEREST: http://www.pinterest.com/authornaomi
GOODREADS: http://bit.ly/1VMIegX
INDIEBOUND: http://bit.ly/1PsB9MR
FICTION FINDER: http://bit.ly/1UOlI5P

ACKNOWLEDGMENTS

To God be the glory . . . He is the author of my life! God gives me the inspiration for each and every book . . . books of family, faith, forgiveness, and grace . . .

When God placed it on my heart to write a light-hearted mystery series, I'm glad I obeyed.

Thanks to my daughter, Rachel, who not only designs my covers, memes, posters (well, you get the picture), but is also an amazing author and inspirational speaker.

Rachel, I couldn't have done it without you!

A big thank you goes out to Pam, my dear friend and founder of S&G Publishing. If not for Pam, I might never have been published!

Last, but by no means least, thank you to my awesome readers, who do so much to encourage me and continue make this series a huge success!

ABOUT THE AUTHOR

Naomi Miller mixes up a batch of intrigue, sprinkled with Amish, Mennonite, and English characters, adding a pinch of mystery—and a dash of romance!

Naomi works full time as an author, blogger and inspirational speaker. She is a member of the American Christian Fiction Writers (ACFW) organization.

When she's not working diligently to finish the next novel in her Sweet Shop Mystery series, Naomi tries to make time for attending workshops and writers conferences. Whenever time permits, Naomi can be found in one of two favorite places—the beach and the mountains.

Naomi's day is spent focusing on her writing, editing, and blogging about her experiences. Naomi loves traveling with her family, singing inspirational/gospel music, taking a daily walk, and witnessing to others of the amazing grace of Jesus Christ.

DON'T MISS THE NEXT BOOK IN THIS SERIES COMING NEXT SPRING!

ABOUT THE PUBLISHER

CHRISTIAN PUBLISHING FOR HIS GLORY

S&G Publishing offers books with messages that honor Jesus Christ to the world! S&G works with Christian authors to bring you the best in "inspirational" fiction and non-fiction.

S&G is proud to publish a variety of Christian fiction genres:
inspirational romance
young reader
young adult
speculative
historical
suspense

Check out our website at

sgpublish.com

MORE FROM
S&G PUBLISHING

JUNIOR AUTHOR SERIES

AUTHOR ENCOURAGEMENT SERIES

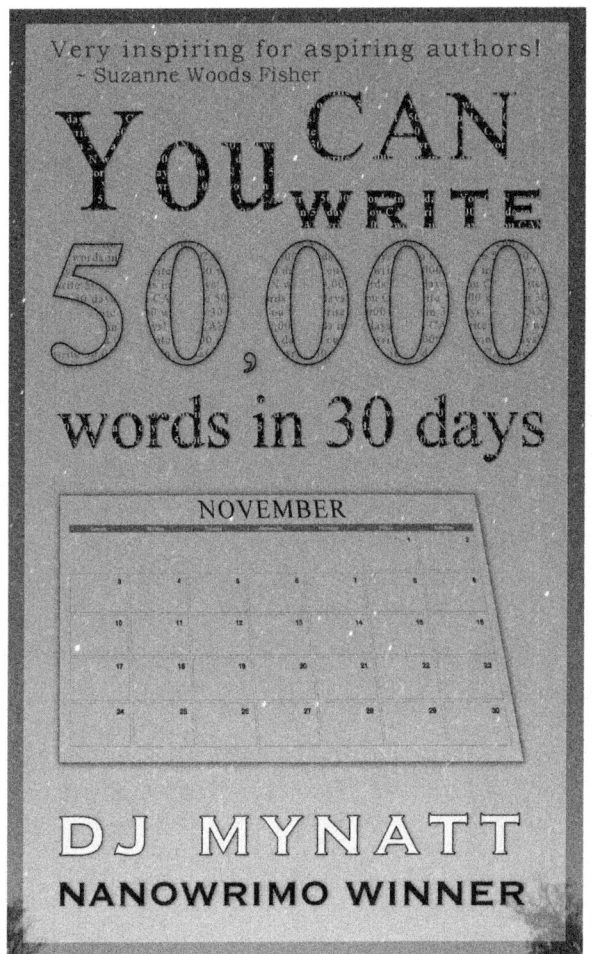

CHECK OUT JC MORROWS'

What if Cinderella had been sent to kill the Prince?

Kayden never thought of herself as the Belle of the ball, but she finds herself in the royal palace, surrounded by society darlings - and the only thing she has in common with them is that they're all vying for the Prince.

They're after his crown. She's after his head.

Kayden's mission should have been simple...
She was sent to kill the Prince...
Not to fall in love with him.

Within the palace walls, Kayden has discovered that things are not as she expected. Is there more to the royal family, or... is there a more sinister depth to Drey's mission?

ORDER OF THE MOONSTONE SERIES:

A Reluctant Assassin has made...
A Treacherous Decision.

Now she and the Prince are desperate to escape... But will the Order of the MoonStone allow it - or will Kayden be forced to choose between the Prince and her former allies ... former friends?

Forced to flee... Wounded... and on the run...

Not exactly a safe place for a former assassin and a prince with a price on his head.
In the dark streets of Auralius, Kayden and her prince struggle to find a way to set the country right again. But the Order of the MoonStone has a long reach and a strong grip.

NEW FROM JC MORROWS

CPSIA information can be obtained
at www.ICGtesting.com
Printed in the USA
LVOW13s1829300118
564592LV00016B/1813/P